SPOTTER'S GUIDE TO
ROCKS & MINERALS

Alan Woolley

Photography by Mike Freeman

Illustrated by Cristina Adami, Jeremy Gower,
Ian Jackson, Luis Rey, Chris Shields, Stuart Trotter

Edited by Fiona Watt, Gill Harvey, Rosemary Hartill
and Sue Jacquemier
Geological advisor : Annette Shelford
Designed by Cristina Adami
Series editor : Philippa Wingate
Cover design and series designer : Laura Fearn

Picture credits : Opal on the cover and rhyolite (p. 43) – The
Natural History Museum, London. Title page – Corbis/Gary
Thomas Sutto. Pages 4-5 – Corbis/Tom Bean. Backgrounds
on pages 1-3 and 6-64 – Digital Vision ©.

First published in 2000 by Usborne Publishing Ltd.,
Usborne House, 83-85 Saffron Hill, London.
EC1N 8RT, England. www.usborne.com.

Printed in Spain.

CONTENTS

HOW TO USE THIS BOOK

This book is an identification guide to many types of minerals, rocks and fossils. It begins by explaining the difference between these three categories, how they are formed, and what the Earth is made of. Descriptions of the individual specimens are arranged with minerals first, rocks next and fossils last. Each specimen has a photograph and a description to help you identify it. There is also a circle to tick if you spot it.

USEFUL WORDS AND SCORECARD
On page 60, there is a list explaining some of the more difficult words that appear in this book.

The scorecard on pages 62 and 63 gives you a score for each mineral, rock, or fossil that you spot.

WHERE TO LOOK

The rocks, minerals and fossils in this book are from all around the world, so a good place to spot them is at a natural history or geological museum.

Many of them occur naturally in Britain and Europe, so look around you when you are out in the country or walking along a beach.

Another good place to look is in towns, as many buildings are built out of rock. Look in shops, too – some sell polished or unpolished minerals and fossils, while others sell jewellery set with different stones. You may also see some interesting examples if you visit tourist attractions, such as underground caves.

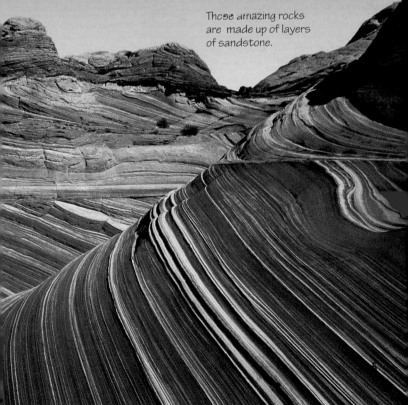

These amazing rocks are made up of layers of sandstone.

STUDYING THE EARTH

The Earth is made up from several layers. The solid outer layer, known as the crust, is relatively thin. It is made up from three different kinds of rocks: igneous, sedimentary and metamorphic. You can find out about these on pages 9-13. The middle layer of the Earth is called the mantle. The central part of the Earth is called the core.

Geologists (scientists who study the Earth and what it is made of) can find out quite easily about the rocks in the crust. They collect samples from the surface and drill into the crust to collect rocks from deeper down.

This picture of the Earth has been cut away to show its layers (not to scale).

It's more difficult to find out about the mantle and the core. Clues about them come from volcanic eruptions which bring molten or melted rock from the mantle to the surface.

Geologists also discover things about the layers by looking at the way earthquake shock waves travel through the Earth.

THE CRUST
is between 5km (3 miles) and 70km (43 miles) thick, and is made up of different types of rock.

THE MANTLE
is about 300km (1,900 miles) thick. It is made of silicon and magnesium. The top and lower parts are solid rock. The middle part has melted to form a substance called magma.

Outer core

Inner core

THE CORE
is probably made of iron and nickel. The outer core is about 2,200km (1,400 miles) thick and is melted rock, whereas the inner core is solid. It is about 1,300km (800 miles) thick.

WHAT ARE MINERALS?

Minerals occur naturally in the Earth, and are the chemical substances that rocks are made of. Minerals, in turn, are made of "elements"– simple substances that cannot be broken down into any other substance. Some minerals, such as gold, are made of only one element, but most are made of two or more.

Granite is a rock made from a mixture of minerals, mainly feldspar, quartz and mica.

The mineral haematite sometimes forms rounded lumps.

RECOGNIZING MINERALS

Many minerals have a particular shape or colour that will help you to identify them. Some form crystals with flat surfaces and regular shapes. Others are found as shapeless lumps or "masses". Some also form crusts on other rocks and minerals.

Amethyst crystals

Smithsonite forms crusts on other rocks.

WHAT ARE ROCKS?

Rocks are usually made up of a mixture of different kinds of minerals. There are three types of rocks: igneous, sedimentary and metamorphic. These are formed in different ways.

This diagram shows where the three different kinds of rocks are formed.

Sedimentary rocks form on sea beds, rivers and lakes.

Igneous rocks are formed from magma (see page 10-11)

Metamorphic rocks are formed when they are heated or crushed by igneous rocks nearby.

IGNEOUS ROCKS

There are two kinds of igneous rock, extrusive and intrusive. They are formed in different ways. Beneath the Earth's crust lies red-hot molten rock, called magma. Magma is a mushy liquid, made up of a mixture of different melted minerals and mineral crystals. During a volcanic eruption, magma is forced through a weakness in the Earth's crust onto the surface. It cools and solidifies to form rock. When magma is forced onto the Earth's surface, it is known as lava. Rocks formed in this way are called extrusive igneous rocks.

The picture below shows molten lava oozing from a volcano.

Other kinds of igneous rocks are formed when magma works its way in between layers of rocks and solidifies before it reaches the surface. These are called intrusive igneous rocks. Intrusive igneous rocks may appear on the Earth's surface if the overlying rocks are worn away.

This diagram shows a batholith, the largest kind of intrusive igneous rock.

Volcano—

Batholith

Layers of ash and lava

SEDIMENTARY ROCKS

Sedimentary rocks are made from fragments of rocks and the remains of animals and plants.

Rain, wind and ice wear away tiny pieces of rock from exposed surfaces, such as these mountains. The fragments are called sediment.

Rain washes the sediment into rivers or streams. The fragments tumble and knock against each other. This grinds them down to form sand and mud. Eventually the sediment is washed into the sea.

On the sea-bed, the sediment builds up in layers along with the remains of sea creatures. In time, the layers are packed down by the weight of the layers on top. Over millions of years, they become solid rock.

METAMORPHIC ROCKS

Metamorphic rocks are formed when sedimentary or igneous rocks are altered by high temperatures or pressure, or both. The heat and pressure change the texture, appearance and chemical composition of the rocks.

Marble is a metamorphic rock formed from limestone.

When magma comes into contact with other rocks, these rocks become metamorphic rocks.

Metamorphic rocks

Sedimentary rocks

Magma

← Some metamorphic rocks are formed when magma is forced into an area of the Earth's crust. The magma heats the surrounding rocks, changing their composition.

➡ Although the Earth's crust appears to be solid, it is actually broken into several enormous pieces, called plates. These plates are constantly moving at a rate of about 50mm (2in) each year. This builds up pressure in the crust, causing rocks to change.

When two plates move together, all the rocks between them are crushed and squeezed.

WHAT ARE FOSSILS?

Fossils are the impressions or remains of animals and plants that have been preserved in rocks (usually sedimentary rocks). When animals and plants die, they often decay or are eaten. Fossils form when they are covered with sand or mud (sediment) before they decay.

Fossils are formed in two ways. They can consist of the actual material of a plant or animal that has been preserved, such as shells or bones; or they can be formed from minerals that filled the space left behind when the animal or plant dissolved away.

1. Millions of years ago ichthyosaurs, like these, lived in the sea.

2. When an ichthyosaur died, its remains sank to the sea-bed.

3. The soft body decayed, but the skeleton was covered in sediment and preserved. The bones were slowly replaced by minerals, and a fossil formed.

Remains of animals that are now extinct have also been found preserved in things other than rocks. In northern Siberia, mammoths have been found preserved in ice. The ice acts like a giant freezer.

Mammoths were larger than elephants and were covered in a hairy coat.

Some fossils, known as trace fossils, are the remains of marks, such as footprints or burrows.

This fossil shows burrows made by tiny worms that lived on the bed of a shallow sea.

Fossils of dinosaur footprints may show details of the skin and deep imprints of the claws.

Whole insects can be found preserved in amber. These insects were trapped in resin which dripped from trees. The resin fossilized, leaving the insect inside.

An insect preserved in amber

MINERALS

← GOLD

Gold is a metal, and an unmixed element. It is usually found as tiny yellow specks, but occasionally forms larger lumps called "nuggets". It occurs in igneous and sedimentary rocks, and is sometimes found in river sand and gravel. It is softer than "fool's gold" (pyrite or chalcopyrite – see pages 17-18).

Because gold is rare, it is considered a symbol of power and wealth.

Flecks of gold glisten in this piece of rock.

➡ SILVER

Silver can be found as small specks and also as wiry shapes. It usually occurs in igneous rocks. It is silver-white, but quickly tarnishes (goes dull and black) when exposed to air. Silver, like gold, is one of the few metals that is found unmixed with other elements.

← SULPHUR

Another unmixed element, found in rocks near volcanoes and around hot springs. It usually makes a powdery crust on rocks, but can also form large crystals. It burns easily, with a strong, unpleasant smell. It is usually bright yellow, but can be brownish.

→ PYRITE

Pyrite is a common mineral, made of iron and sulphur. It is also called iron pyrites, or fool's gold, because of its pale brassy yellow colour. It is actually a paler yellow than real gold. Many fossils are made of pyrite. It forms crystals, particularly cube-shaped ones. It also forms nodules (rounded lumps) in some rocks, such as shale and chalk.

A single cube-shaped pyrite crystal

17

MINERALS

◀ CHALCOPYRITE

Chalcopyrite is sometimes called copper pyrites and, like pyrite, is also known as fool's gold. It is made of the elements copper, iron and sulphur, and is found in a wide range of metamorphic and igneous rocks. It forms irregular lumps, and sometimes crystals.
It is brass-yellow, but will tarnish and look iridescent (how oil looks on water, with shimmering reds, blues and purples).

➡ GALENA

Galena is made of the elements lead and sulphur. It often forms cube-shaped crystals.
It is found in some sedimentary rocks, and often with pyrite, sphalerite, and chalcopyrite. When it is freshly split it is a shining silver-grey, but it tarnishes to dull grey with time.

➡ SPHALERITE

Sphalerite is also known as zinc blende, blende or black jack. It often occurs with galena and can easily be mistaken for other minerals. It varies from brown to black, but can be yellow and sometimes transparent. It is the source of most of the world's zinc.

⬅ ARSENOPYRITE

Arsenopyrite also has the strange name of mispickel. It is made of sulphur, iron and arsenic, and is often found with gold and quartz. It may form crystals. Arsenopyrite is silver to greyish-white, and may have a brownish tarnish.

19

MINERALS

➡ GRAPHITE

Graphite is made of the element carbon. It is often found in schist, a kind of metamorphic rock, and limestone, a sedimentary rock, most commonly as tiny grains but sometimes as flat crystals. The name comes from the Greek word *graphos*, which means "to write".

The "lead" in pencils is not lead at all, but a mixture of clay and graphite.

⬇ DIAMOND

Like graphite, diamond is made of carbon. It occurs mainly in a rock called kimberlite. Not all diamonds are clear – they can be yellow, red, black or brown. It is the hardest mineral known.

Natural diamonds do not sparkle. They only sparkle when they are cut and light shines through them.

➡ CORUNDUM

This mineral is made of aluminium and oxygen. It is found mainly in metamorphic rocks. It forms crystals of different shapes. These can be brown, yellow or green, but the best-known kinds are red and blue (see below). Corundum is very hard and is used to make the rough surface on emery boards and sandpaper.

Uncut ruby

◀ SAPPHIRE and RUBY

These are varieties of corundum. Sapphire is pale blue and transparent, while ruby is pink to blood-red and is also transparent. Together with diamonds and emeralds, these are the most precious gemstones.

Rubies

Sapphire

21

MINERALS

◀ GOETHITE

Goethite often forms rounded lumps or long, sausage-like masses. It is called a secondary mineral, which means a mineral that is formed by the alteration of other minerals. Goethite is nearly always formed by the effect of water on minerals such as magnetite and pyrite. It is usually very dark brown, but may be yellow-brown.

➡ PYROLUSITE

Pyrolusite is made of manganese and oxygen. It often forms fern-like shapes in sedimentary rocks. These are called dendrites and are often mistaken for fossil leaves. It also forms masses of thin crystals. Large crystals are rare. Nodules (rounded lumps) of pyrolusite are found on the sea-bed.

Halite
crystals

← HALITE

Halite is also called "rock salt", but it is best known as the table salt you eat. It was formed thousands of years ago by the evaporation of sea water. Thick layers of it are found in sedimentary rock.

Halite is usually found in masses (see page 8), but it can also be found as single, cube-shaped crystals. It is transparent or white in its purest form, but is usually stained brown or yellow.

➡ FLUORITE

Fluorite is also called fluorspar. It forms cubed-shaped crystals that are often blue, violet, purple, green or yellow, though white or pink types are sometimes found, too. In ultra-violet light, it glows with an effect called fluorescence, which is named after fluorite.

MINERALS

➡ CALCITE
Calcite is made of calcium, carbon and oxygen. It is usually white, but can be grey, green, yellow, red or blue. When it is broken, it forms six-sided shapes, called rhombs. This is the mineral that forms "fur" inside kettles.

Crystalline calcite

Dogstooth calcite

Iceland spar. Anything looked at through this type of calcite appears as double.

Limestone and marble are made mostly of calcite. Stalactites and stalagmites (see page 48) are formed when water containing a type of calcite drips from the roof of a cave in limestone areas.

24

← MALACHITE

Malachite is made of copper, carbon, oxygen and hydrogen. The copper gives it its colour – it is bright green with bands of lighter and darker shades of green. The bands can be clearly seen when it is cut and polished. It is often used in jewellery.

A piece of polished malachite, showing the banded patterns

→ SMITHSONITE

Smithsonite is made of zinc, carbon and oxygen. It can be white, grey, green, blue, yellow, purple or brown. Its tiny crystals form bubbly looking rounded masses. It also forms crusts, coating other minerals and rocks.

MINERALS

← BARYTE

Crystals of baryte are quite common. They tend to be white, but may be tinged with yellow, brown or red. Baryte is often glassy-looking and transparent, and is often found in the holes between layers of limestone. It contains the element barium, which gives the bright green colour in flares and fireworks.

→ GYPSUM

Gypsum is generally white, but may be shades of grey, yellow or pink. It sometimes forms clear crystals, called selenite. You may see it as alabaster, a fine-grained form of gypsum that is carved into ornaments, bowls and other objects.

➡ APATITE

Your teeth are made mostly of apatite, and so are your bones. A sedimentary rock called phosphate rock is made almost entirely of apatite, and is mined for use as a fertilizer. Pure apatite is made mainly of calcium and phosphorous, and may be pale green, blue-green, white or brown.

Apatite crystals

A polished piece of turquoise

⬅ TURQUOISE

Turquoise is made mainly of copper, aluminium and phosphorous. Its colour varies from sky-blue to apple green, which makes it popular as a gemstone. It is usually found in hot, dry regions as masses or as a crust. Crystals are small and very rare.

27

MINERALS

An uncut garnet

A cut and polished garnet

◀ GARNET
Garnet is a mixture of several elements, and there are many different kinds. It forms crystals, which are often dark red and red-brown, but can also be green. They are common in some metamorphic rocks. Garnets are frequently used to make jewellery.

➡ TOURMALINE
Tourmaline forms long crystals which have parallel lines running along their length. If you look at right angles to these lines, you will see that they form a roughly triangular shape. Tourmaline is often black, but blue, pink and green crystals also occur.

➤ OLIVINE

Olivine is made of magnesium, iron, silicon and oxygen. It usually forms grainy masses. It is often olive-green, but some kinds are white and others black. When it is green and transparent it is called peridot, and may be used as a gemstone.

◀ SERPENTINE

Serpentine is a common mineral that is usually green, but may be yellow or grey. It can be striped or speckled. It is found as irregular lumps, or as thin fibres, a bit like cotton wool. These fibres are known as asbestos. The dust from asbestos is very bad for your health.

MINERALS

➡ BERYL

Beryl is made of the elements silicon, oxygen, aluminium and beryllium. It usually forms long crystals with six sides. Transparent beryl is known by different names. As well as aquamarine and emerald (see below), there is a yellow type called heliodor and a pink type called morganite.

Emerald

Aquamarine

⬅ EMERALD and AQUAMARINE

These are varieties of beryl. Emerald is a transparent dark green or light green gemstone, most commonly found in Colombia. Aquamarine is the name for pale blue-green beryl. Emerald is rarer than aquamarine, and therefore, a much more valuable gemstone.

➡ AUGITE

Augite is made up mainly of calcium, magnesium, aluminium, iron and silicon. It forms short, fat column-shaped crystals with eight sides. In colour, it ranges from black to dark green. Augite is principally found in basalts and other types of igneous rocks.

⬅ HORNBLENDE

Hornblende is made up of a wide variety of elements. It forms fairly large crystals. These are column-shaped, and can be short or long. They vary from green to black. Hornblende is found in a wide range of igneous and metamorphic rocks, and forms a large part of a rock called amphibolite.

MINERALS

➡ MICA

There are two main kinds of mica – biotite is black or brown and shiny, and muscovite is white and silvery. Both are made up of thin sheets or flakes. When separated, these layers are so thin they are transparent. Both types are common in granites, pegmatites and schists (different kinds of igneous and metamorphic rocks).

Biotite

Muscovite

⬅ TALC

Talc is made of silicon, magnesium, oxygen and hydrogen. It is the softest mineral known. You can scratch it easily with a fingernail. It is usually pale green, but may be white or grey. Talc is used to make talcum powder. Some rocks, called soapstone or steatite, are made almost entirely of talc.

QUARTZ

Quartz is made of silicon and oxygen. It is found in igneous, sedimentary and metamorphic rocks. There are many varieties, some of which are described over the next few pages. The crystals are usually six-sided, and can be found in a range of different colours.

Rock crystal

Milky quartz

Shapes of some perfect quartz crystals

↑ MILKY QUARTZ and ROCK CRYSTAL

The most common variety of quartz is the opaque, white kind, called milky quartz. Clear transparent quartz is called rock crystal and is sometimes mistaken for diamonds. It is found as crystals or small irregular lumps.

33

MINERALS

➡ AMETHYST

Amethyst is another type of quartz. It is transparent and varies in colour from deep purple to pale blue. It is popular as a semi-precious stone and is often set in jewellery. It forms crystals that can be found as crusts lining holes in volcanic rocks.

⬅ SMOKY QUARTZ

Smoky quartz forms transparent to translucent crystals, with six sides. They range from smoky-brown to nearly black in colour. Smoky quartz is sometimes known as cairngorm, after the Cairngorm mountains in Scotland where it is found.

◄ CHALCEDONY

This is another variety of quartz. It is very fine-grained and does not form crystals, usually forming rounded masses instead. There are many varieties of chalcedony (see below). It varies from white to grey, but may also be red, brown or black.

➡ TYPES OF CHALCEDONY

Different kinds of chalcedony include carnelian, sard, jasper, chrysoprase and heliotrope, all of which are used in jewellery. Carnelian and sard are red or reddish brown. Jasper is opaque and usually dark red, but may be yellow or brown. Chrysoprase is apple-green, while heliotrope or "bloodstone" is green with red spots that look like blood.

A polished piece of carnelian

MINERALS

➡ AGATE

Agate is a kind of quartz made up of many coloured bands. Most agate occurs in rounded lumps, which vary from the size of a marble to that of a football. The middle of the agate may consist of rock crystal. The bands vary from milky white to green, brown, red and black. If the bands are straight, it is called onyx.

⬅ OPAL

Opal is made of silicon, oxygen and water. It varies in colour from clear to translucent milky white, grey, blue, green, red, brown or black. Precious opal often has a variety of iridescent blues, reds and yellows. In fire opal, red and yellow colours make fire-like reflections.

Opal is often polished and set in jewellery.

A polished piece of opal

← ORTHOCLASE FELDSPAR

Feldspars are minerals made up of a variety of elements, and they form a large part of igneous rocks. Orthoclase feldspar forms stubby four- and six-sided crystals that range in colour from milky white to pale pink. The white or pink grains that you see in polished granite are usually orthoclase.

→ PLAGIOCLASE FELDSPAR

Plagioclase feldspar can form flat crystals, but it is much more commonly found as an irregular mass. It occurs in a wide range of igneous rocks. One type, called labradorite, is often striking in colour with a variety of iridescent blues and greens.

Labradorite, a type of plagioclase feldspar

MINERALS

◄ MAGNETITE
Magnetite is made of iron and oxygen. It forms black crystals, the same shape as natural diamond crystals (see page 20). It is strongly magnetic, so if you put it near a compass it will make the needle move.

➡ HAEMATITE
Like magnetite, haematite is made of iron and oxygen, but in different proportions. Haematite is named after the Greek word for blood, as it often ranges from dull to bright red, but it can be steel-grey or black. It is also known as kidney ore because of its shape. It is often found in sedimentary rocks,

IGNEOUS ROCKS

← TUFF

Tuff is made up from small pieces of volcanic rock and crystals cemented together into hard rock. It is built up, layer by layer, from the ash formed by a succession of volcanic explosions. In coarse-grained tuffs, you can see the individual rounded pieces of rock, together with broken crystals of minerals.

→ AGGLOMERATE

This is made of large lumps of volcanic rock, such as basalt, which have been thrown out of a volcano by violent eruptions. The lumps are at least six centimetres across, and can be many metres wide. They may be pieces of rock from inside a volcano, or "bombs" – pieces of lava which have cooled as they were hurled through the air.

Some volcanic bombs form a "tail" as they twist through the air.

IGNEOUS ROCKS

← GRANITE
Granite is a coarse-grained igneous rock. It can be white, grey or pink, and is usually mottled because of the different minerals it contains. The main minerals are feldspar, quartz and mica. Granite is often polished, then used as a decorative building stone.

→ PEGMATITE
This is a very coarse rock which contains large crystals. The main minerals are feldspar, quartz and mica (particularly muscovite), but there may be hundreds of others too. Because the crystals in pegmatites are so large, they are some of the best rocks for studying lots of different minerals.

➡ GABBRO

This is a coarse-grained rock with an even texture. It is usually greenish dark grey or black, and is often speckled with minerals, such as plagioclase feldspar, augite and olivine. It is an extrusive igneous rock (see pages 10-11) that has cooled slowly, allowing large crystals to grow.

⬅ SERPENTINITE

This is made mainly of the mineral serpentine. It is often patchy, streaky and veined, with tiny fibres of serpentine running across the veins. It is usually dark green, but may have black, white or even red patches and streaks. Surfaces that are exposed to the weather may be red-brown.

IGNEOUS ROCKS

← OBSIDIAN
Obsidian is natural glass, formed when magma from a volcano cools very rapidly. It cools so quickly that crystals rarely have time to form. It is usually shiny and black, but can be grey or red-brown. Obsidian breaks easily into pieces with sharp edges and smooth rounded surfaces.

➡ PUMICE
Pumice is full of tiny gas bubbles, so it is very light and will often float on water. It tends to be grey, but may be yellowish. Pumice is formed when magma containing bubbles of gas reaches the Earth's surface. Then, if the magma cools quickly, the bubbles are preserved in the rock. Pumice is often used as an abrasive for making things smooth.

➡ RHYOLITE

Rhyolite is similar to granite, but has finer grains. It may contain a few large crystals of feldspar or quartz. It is white or grey, but can also be reddish or black. It may also have bands running through it. These were caused by layers of lava flowing from a volcano.

⬅ BASALT

This is a fine- to medium- grained rock that ranges in colour from black to dark grey. It is volcanic, and may form lava flows that cover huge areas. It also builds up to form volcanos. When thick flows of basalt lava cool down, they often break into six-sided columns.

SEDIMENTARY ROCKS

Sandstone

Ripple marks on a slab of sandstone

Grit

⬆ SANDSTONE and GRIT

Sandstone and grit are made of grains of sand usually held together by calcite or a substance called silica. The grains are often quartz, but can be feldspar or other minerals. If the grains are angular, rather than smooth and round, the rock is called a grit. The colour of both sandstone and grit may be yellow, red, white or greenish, depending on where they were formed. Most deposits of sand were formed in the sea, carried there by rivers. For this reason, ripple marks, like those seen on sandy beaches when the tide goes out, are quite commonly found in sandstones. Sandstone is also found in deserts. It is formed from sand blown there by the wind. This type of sandstone is usually red.

➡ SILTSTONE

Siltstone is formed from compacted "silt". Silt is sediment which is finer-grained than sand but coarser than mud. Sometimes you can see the glint of tiny mica flakes in it, or larger grains of feldspar or quartz. It is often pale to dark grey in colour. Fossils are common in siltstone.

⬅ MUDSTONE and SHALE

These rocks are formed from the hardening of fine mud in the sea. If the rock has many fine layers, it is called shale; if not, it is called mudstone. Both are often black to dark grey in colour, but may be brown, red or green. They often contain fossils, which are preserved as the mineral pyrite.

SEDIMENTARY ROCKS

Limestone containing fossils of shells

➡ LIMESTONE
Limestone is a common sedimentary rock made up mainly of the mineral calcite. The calcite may have very fine grains, or it may form crystals 10mm (½ in) or more across. It is often layered, though the layers can be hard to spot.

Limestone is often greyish white in colour, but may be black, dark grey or reddish. It can be formed almost totally from the shells and bones of sea creatures, and fossils are often found in it. Some imestone can consist of whole coral reefs that have fossilized.

Limestone containing a variety of fossils

➡ CHALK

Chalk is a very fine-grained type of limestone, made up of the skeletons of tiny sea animals. Fossils of creatures such as sea urchins are often found in it. It is usually pure white, showing how clear the seas were when it was formed, but it can be stained brown or yellow. Chalk is usually porous, which means It absorbs liquid.

⬅ OOLITE

This limestone is made of tiny ball-shaped grains called ooliths, usually about 1-2mm across. Grains of quartz sand and fragments of shell and other fossils may be among them. It is usually yellow to white, but can be brown or red. Ooliths are formed as layers of calcite build up around grains of sand that are being rolled along the sea bed by the sea's currents.

SEDIMENTARY ROCKS

➡ STALACTITES and STALAGMITES

Both stalactites and stalagmites are found in limestone areas. Stalactites hang from the roofs of caves, while stalagmites grow up from the floor. They are formed when water containing dissolved calcite drips down, leaving a small amount of calcite behind.

Stalactite

Stalagmite

⬅ TRAVERTINE and TUFA

These are both formed from calcite dissolved in water. They contain lots of holes and cavities, so they look spongy. Both rocks can be reddish, white or yellow. Travertine is found around hot springs and geysers, while tufa occurs in limestone caves and around springs.

Travertine

➡ FLINT NODULES

Flint nodules (often just called flints) are made of chalcedony and form rounded lumps that separate easily from the rocks around them. They are often found in chalk, and are usually white on the outside and black inside. Flints are often the size of a potato but can be much bigger. They may be spherical or sausage-shaped.

← PYRITE NODULES

These nodules are made of the mineral pyrite. They are found in sedimentary rocks, such as chalk, siltstone and shale. The nodules are made up from long thin pyrite crystals, which radiate outwards from the middle of the nodule. They are brown or black outside, with a shining yellow inside.

SEDIMENTARY ROCKS

➡ CONGLOMERATE

Conglomerate is made up of rounded fragments with a sandy material in between. It is formed from material washed down rivers and along coastlines. The fragments may be of any hard rock, and range in size from small pebbles to boulders. It varies in colour, depending on the type of rocks that it is made up of.

⬅ BRECCIA

Breccia, like conglomerate, is made of fragments of rock held together by a finer sandy material. In breccia, the fragments are angular. This shows that they were not carried far by water, as this would have rounded them. Fragments vary from pebbles to boulders, and may consist of almost any type of rock.

METAMORPHIC ROCKS

➡ MARBLE
Marble is made mainly
of the mineral calcite.
It is a metamorphic
rock formed by heat
or pressure on
limestone. It can
be white, light
brown or grey, but
also black, green,
or red. The word
"marble" is
sometimes used
for other rocks,
such as alabaster.

⬅ QUARTZITE
This is made mainly
of grains of quartz,
but it may contain
feldspar, mica or
other minerals, too.
Quartzite is
metamorphosed
quartz sandstone. It
has an even texture
and the quartz
grains are closely
packed together.
It is often white, but
may be yellowish,
grey or reddish.

51

METAMORPHIC ROCKS

➡ SLATE

Slate is formed by the metamorphism of shale and mudstone. It is made of tiny grains of minerals, such as mica, which are too small to be seen with the naked eye. It can be split easily into thin sheets, along surfaces known as cleavage planes. It may be black, red, greenish or purple.

⬅ PHYLLITE

Like slate, phyllite is made of metamorphosed shale and mudstone. Phyllite has been heated and squeezed more than slate, so the minerals it contains are coarser. Phyllite splits easily into sheets and slabs, revealing a surface that is usually shiny. It is green to silver-grey in colour.

➡ MICA SCHIST

Schists are mainly metamorphosed siltstone and mudstone. Mica schist is composed mainly of mica (biotite or muscovite, or both) along with some quartz and feldspar. If it is made of muscovite, it tends to be silvery grey and sparkling. If it is mainly biotite, it may be brown or black.

⬅ GARNET SCHIST

This is like mica schist, but it also contains garnets. Garnets are often dark red, though they can be green or white. They are rounded in shape and vary in size. The rock splits easily due to the mica it contains. It occurs with other metamorphic rocks, such as mica schist, phyllite and amphibolite.

METAMORPHIC ROCKS

➡ AMPHIBOLITE

This is a medium- to coarse-grained rock made mostly of the mineral hornblende. Amphibolite is usually black or dark green and is often banded with dark and light layers. It is formed mainly from metamorphosed igneous rocks, such as basalt.

⬅ GNEISS

Gneiss is made mostly of feldspar, mica (biotite or muscovite) and quartz. The feldspar may form large pink or white crystals that look like eyes. Gneiss is often formed at a very high temperature – it may even partly melt. This results in dark and light layers that alternate in wavy, swirling folds.

FOSSILS

Fossilized
leaves

← FOSSIL PLANTS

Fossil plants are usually
found in fine-grained
sedimentary rock, such as
mudstone and shale.
Some date from about
300 million years ago.
Some of the best-
preserved plant fossils are
leaves and twigs, found in
rocks formed between 65
and 1.8 million years ago.

Single fossil coral

➡ CORAL

Coral consists
of simple
animals with
skeletons made
of calcite. They
are often
preserved as fossils.
Coral fossils may be
single or in groups, called
colonies. Fossils of animals
that lived in the coral,
such as gastropods and
bivalves (see page 56), are
often found with the coral.

A colony of
fossilized coral

FOSSILS

➡ GASTROPODS

These are commonly known as snails. Their shells are usually coiled in spirals. Their fossils are found in shales, mudstones and limestones formed as far back as 540 million years ago.

Three different kinds of gastropods

Two different bivalves

◀ BIVALVES

These include cockles, mussels and razor shells. Their shells are made of two separate parts, called valves, that are hinged together so the animals inside can open them up to feed and close them for protection. Their fossils are found in shales, limestones and mudstones.

➡ BRACHIOPODS

Like bivalves, brachiopods have a hinged pair of shells, but the two are a different size and shape, so that one overlaps the other. Their fossils are found in shales, limestones and mudstone, especially those formed between 500 and 285 million years ago.

Some brachiopods' shells have grooves and ridges.

⬅ ECHINOIDS (sea urchins)

These are rounded or heart-shaped animals up to 100mm (4in) across. The shell is made of plates of calcite, often covered with lumps. On modern-day sea urchins, spines are attached to these lumps, but the spines are rarely preserved in fossils. Echinoids are found in rocks, especially chalk, that were formed less than 200 million years ago.

Echinoid fossil with lumps, showing where the spines used to be

Heart-shaped echinoid fossil

A modern-day sea urchin with spines

FOSSILS

➡ AMMONITES

These were creatures which swam freely in the sea, buoyed up by air inside their shell. They are now extinct. Their fossils are flat spirals and are found in rocks formed 245 to 65 million years ago.

A living ammonite may have looked like this Nautilus, which is found in tropical seas today.

Belemnite fossils are often found broken.

A living belemnite may have looked like this.

⬅ BELEMNITES

Belemnites are extinct sea creatures that looked a little bit like squids. Belemnite fossils are the remains of part of their insides. They are bullet-shaped with a pointed end, and may vary in size, from the length and thickness of a match to 10cm (4in) long.

➡ TRILOBITES

Trilobites were sea creatures that appear in rocks that were formed between 500 to 300 million years ago. Their bodies consisted of a head, bodysegments and tail. It is the head and tail that are usually found as fossils. They are mainly found in siltstones and mudstones.

A complete trilobite may have looked like this.

The fossilized outlines of two tribolytes

A shark's head showing the triangular teeth

⬅ FISH TEETH

Rays and sharks have soft bodies which do not fossilize well, but their teeth do. Most fossilized teeth are triangular, and are most commonly found in rocks formed between 65 and 144 million years ago.

USEFUL WORDS

abrasive – something rough that is used to smooth down other surfaces.

cavities – holes or hollows in solid rock.

cement – minerals that behave like glue, binding other minerals and rocks together.

cleavage – the direction in which some rocks and minerals split apart.

crust – a thin outer coating on a rock or mineral.

crystal – a naturally occurring solid substance with flat surfaces.

deposit – something that builds up gradually, which has been left behind by another substance, for example sediment carried in water.

element – one of the simple substances of which all matter is made. An element cannot be broken down into a simpler substance.

gemstone – a valuable mineral that is hard and rare, such as diamond.

geyser – a hole in the ground through which hot water and steam emerge.

iridescent – having different colours that shimmer and change according to the way you look at them.

mass – a lump of rock or mineral that does not have a definite shape.

massive – the word that describes a mass.

nodule – a rounded lump of mineral found in sedimentary rocks.

opaque – not letting light travel through, not transparent.

sediment – animal remains, and tiny fragments worn away from rock surfaces by rain, ice and wind.

translucent – allows light to travel through, but not clear, like glass.

transparent – easy to see through.

vein – a thin layer of rock or mineral between larger layers of a different rock or mineral.

WEß SITES TO VISIT

If you have access to the Internet, try looking at these Web sites. They will give you information about rocks, minerals and fossils.

Rockwatch – an on-line club for young geologists
http://earthlines.com/rockwatch/

The Geological Society – the society's Web site includes information and resources about rocks, minerals and fossils.
http://www.geolsoc.org.uk/

The Essential Guide to Rocks – part of the BBC Online site. Includes spectacular animation and an interactive timeline.
http://www.bbc.co.uk/education/rocks

Fossil Zone (Discovery Channel Online) – fun, interactive site about dinosaurs and fossils.
http://www.discovery.com/exp/fossilzone/fossilzone.html

Zoom.Dinosaurs.com – excellent information on dinosaurs and fossils. Includes a dinosaur dictionary, information on individual species and a geological timeline.
http//www.zoomdinosaurs.com/

Junior Rockhound Geological Magazine – an on-line magazine which includes information on identifying and collecting rocks, minerals and fossils.
http://www.canadianrockhound.com/junior.html

The San Diego Natural History Museum – go on a dinosaur dig or hunt for fossils on this interactive museum site.
http://www.sdnhm.org/kids/kids.html

Volcano World – a site with up-to-date information on volcanic eruptions. Try the activities in Kid's Door, too.
http://volcano.und.nodak.edu/

SCORECARD

The rocks and minerals on this scorecard are in alphabetical order. When you spot one fill in the date, beside its name. A common one scores 5, a rare one is worth 25.

At the end of a day's spotting, add up all the points you have scored on a sheet of paper and keep a record of them. See if you can you score more points another day?

Name of rock or mineral	Score	Date spotted	Name of rock or mineral	Score	Date spotted
Agate	15		Chalcopyrite	20	
Agglomerate	25		Chalk	15	
Amethyst	20		Conglomerate	20	
Ammonites	15		Coral	20	
Amphibolite	25		Corundum	15	
Apatite	20		Crystalline calcite	10	
Aquamarine	10		Diamond	10	
Arsenopyrite	25		Dogstooth calcite	15	
Augite	20		Echinoids	20	
Baryte	25		Emerald	10	
Basalt	15		Fish teeth	25	
Belemnites	20		Flint nodules	10	
Beryl	20		Fluorite	15	
Biotite	15		Fossil plants	20	
Bivalves	15		Gabbro	25	
Brachiopods	15		Galena	20	
Breccia	25		Garnet	10	
Carnelian	20		Garnet schist	25	
Chalcedony	25		Gastropods	20	

Name of rock or mineral	Score	Date spotted	Name of rock or mineral	Score	Date spotted
Gneiss	20		Pumice	25	
Goethite	25		Pyrite	15	
Gold	5		Pyrite nodules	15	
Granite	15		Pyrolusite	25	
Graphite	5		Quartzite	20	
Grit	10		Rhyolite	20	
Gypsum	15		Rock crystal	15	
Halite	5		Ruby	10	
Haematite	15		Sandstone	10	
Hornblende	20		Sapphire	10	
Limestone	15		Serpentine	15	
Magnetite	20		Serpentinite	20	
Malachite	20		Siltstone	15	
Marble	10		Silver	5	
Mica schist	20		Slate	5	
Milky quartz	10		Smithsonite	25	
Mudstone & shale	10		Smoky quartz	25	
Muscovite	15		Sphalerite	20	
Obsidian	25		Stalactites & Stalagmites	25	
Olivine	20		Sulphur	15	
Oolite	25		Talc	10	
Opal	15		Tourmaline	20	
Orthoclase feldspar	15		Travertine & Tufa	25	
Pegmatite	25		Trilobites	25	
Phyllite	20		Tuff	20	
Plagioclase feldspar	15		Turquoise	15	

INDEX